Elizabeth McKay & Maria Bogade

Wee Granny
and the
Ceilidh

Ceilidh "kay-lee" is a Gaelic word for a
Scottish country dance

To Olivia and Matthew, with love – E. M.

To my children, for adding a wee bit of magic
to my everyday adventures – M. B.

Picture Kelpies is an imprint of Floris Books. First published in 2015 by
Floris Books. Text © 2015 Elizabeth McKay. Illustrations © 2015 Maria Bogade
Elizabeth McKay and Maria Bogade assert their right under the Copyright,
Designs and Patent Act 1988 to be identified as the Author and Illustrator
of this Work. All rights reserved. No part of this publication may be reproduced
without prior permission of Floris Books, 15 Harrison Gardens, Edinburgh
www.florisbooks.co.uk. The publisher acknowledges subsidy from
Creative Scotland towards the publication of this volume. British Library CIP
Data available. ISBN 978-178250-209-8. Printed in China

This book belongs to

_____

_____

_____

It was the day of the school ceilidh and Emily and Harry were practising their Scottish dancing. Mum had gone on ahead to set up, and they were waiting to take the bus with Wee Granny. They hoped she'd bring her tartan bag. Amazing things always happened when Wee Granny brought her bag.

Once, when they were playing football in the park, Harry kicked the ball so hard it landed in a tree. Wee Granny reached into her tartan bag and pulled out...

...a ladder, so she could climb up and get the ball!

"Wee Granny," Harry said while they were waiting for the bus, "have you got anything exciting in your bag today?"

"Just my bus pass," said Wee Granny, "and a few other bits and pieces."

Then they heard a *ting ting!*

"Someone's sending me a message," Wee Granny said, reaching into her bag and bringing out...

...a desk and a computer!

"It's an email from your mum," Wee Granny said. "She's asked us to buy more lemonade and crisps for the school ceilidh."

The shop was on the other side of the road, but there were so many cars rushing past it was impossible to cross.

"One moment," said Wee Granny, reaching inside her tartan bag. The children could hardly believe their eyes when she brought out...

...a set of traffic lights!

"Wait for the green man, my bonnie darlings,"
said Wee Granny, making sure it was safe to cross.

"Are you sure you'll manage to carry everything, Wee Granny?" asked Mr Gordon in the shop.

"Yes, thank you, Mr Gordon" said Wee Granny, "There's plenty of room inside my bag. I don't have a lot in it today."

As they left the shop, they saw their bus pulling away.

"Oh no, we've missed the bus! We'll be late!" cried Emily.

"Don't worry, my bonnie darlings," said Wee Granny. "I've got the very thing to get us there in time."

"Have you got a bus inside your bag, Wee Granny?" asked Harry.

"What a funny thing to say, Harry." Wee Granny giggled. "Of course I don't have a bus inside my bag."

The children were disappointed.

"You need a special licence to drive a bus," Wee Granny said. "But I do have..."

"A motorbike!" said Emily.

"With a side-car!" said Harry.

Wee Granny reached into her tartan bag again and brought out four helmets and four pairs of goggles.

"Fasten your seatbelts, my bonnie darlings," said Wee Granny,
"and let's *gooooooo*."

They vroomed past the bakery, the playground, and the ice-cream shop! And then they turned a corner and screeched to a sudden stop.

A fire engine was blocking their path and great fountains of water were shooting up into the air.

"I'm sorry, Wee Granny," said a very wet fireman. "There's a burst pipe and the road ahead is flooded. You can't go any further."

But Wee Granny had an idea.

"I don't know why I didn't think of it before," she said, opening her tartan bag, and pulling and pulling until out came…

...a multi-coloured hot-air balloon.

"It'll just take a minute to inflate," said Wee Granny.

But before the children could climb into the basket they saw someone striding towards them.

"Oi," shouted the traffic warden. "You can't leave your motorbike there!"

"Quick, my bonnie darlings," said Wee Granny, "we'd better put the motorbike away. I can't afford to get another parking ticket."

Wee Granny opened her tartan bag and in went the goggles, the helmets, the bike and finally the side-car.

Soon they were drifting gently across the pale blue sky. They watched the town below get smaller and smaller as the balloon soared higher and higher towards the fluffy white clouds.

"I can see the school," Emily called out. "It's over there!"

Suddenly there was a strong gust of wind.
  The balloon swished to the right and a gaggle
of geese honked and dived out of the way.
  Then it swooshed to the left and nearly
crashed into a church steeple.

And then it whooshed back and
almost got tangled up in a tall tree.

"It's getting a wee bit choppy,"
called Harry. "I hope we land
soon."

"Me too," yelled Emily. "I'm
starting to feel sick."

"Don't worry, my bonnie
darlings," said Wee Granny,
"I have something that will help."

She opened her bag and
brought out...

"Sweeties?" said Harry.

"I don't see how they can help," said Emily.

"I always find chewing a treacle toffee helps me to relax," said Wee Granny.

She was still rummaging in her bag. "I knew this would come in handy one day," she said, hauling out a huge ship's anchor and dropping it over the side of the basket.

The balloon immediately began falling from the sky. The children closed their eyes when they saw the school playground rising up to meet them. There was a bump, then a thump and finally a crash.

"Here we are, my bonnie darlings," said Wee Granny. "I told you I'd get us to the school in time."

"Thank you for bringing the extra refreshments, Wee Granny," said Mrs Graham, the teacher, "but I'm afraid we're going to have to cancel the ceilidh."

"The band hasn't got any instruments," explained Mum. "The van carrying them is stuck in the flooded streets."

"Och, don't worry about that," said Wee Granny, reaching into her tartan bag and pulling out...

"A guitar... an accordian... a fiddle... drums... a recorder... and bagpipes!" said Emily.

"Please can I play the bagpipes, Wee Granny?" asked Harry.
"Mum won't let me practise at home."
Harry joined the band and they all began to play.
"Now that's what I call music," said Wee Granny.

"Are you having fun, Wee Granny?" asked Emily.

"Oh yes, my bonnie darling," said Wee Granny. "It reminds me of when I was a lassie."

"Wee Granny," said Emily, "Tell us, is your bag magic?"

"Of course not my bonnie darling," said Wee Granny with a wink. "Whatever gave you that idea?"